E - 6   Peterson, Hans.
            The big snowstorm.

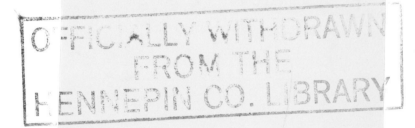

Coward, McCann & Geoghegan, Inc.

New York

The Big
SNOWSTORM

by Hans Peterson

illustrated by Harald Wiberg

translated by Eric Bibb

Coward, McCann & Geoghegan, Inc. New York

English translation text copyright © 1975 by Eric Bibb
First American Edition 1975

illustrations copyright © 1975 by Harald Wiberg
Published simultaneously in Canada by Longman Canada Limited, Toronto.

SBN: GB 698-20347-x   SBN: TR 698-30599-x

Library of Congress Catalog Card Number: 75-7675

It was the end of January
when the big snowstorm came.
Grandma had felt it coming.
"We're in for a storm," she said. "A terrible storm."
The rest of us thought it was too cold to snow.

When I went out to see after Daisy,
who would soon have her calf,
it was at least twenty below.

When I came out of the barn into the moonlight,
I heard the wolves howling way off in the forest.
It sounded horrible.
But when I turned around,
I thought I saw an elf
and right away I felt a little calmer.

I went back to the big house.
Grandma was on the girls' bed taking a little nap.
Father was busy fixing some tool, and
Mother was weaving at the loom. Old Gertrude,
our maid, told stories to Karen and Betsy,
while she darned stockings as usual.

John and Allen, my big brothers, were out in the
bunkhouse with the hired help.
They live there with little-helper Nathan.

I was just about to begin studying my lessons
in the poor light from the oil lamp
when a knock came at the door.

The wolves followed like black shadows.
Jesse ran and ran and ran.
He knew that if he stopped or fell,
it would be all over.
The wolves would be on top of him.
Finally he saw the weak light of our oil lamp and
made it to our door.
We fixed a place in the corner of the big house for
Jesse to spend the night.

The next morning the weather was milder.
Father didn't think it was more than two below.

His face was a little worried, and he looked up in the
sky for signs of snow when we went out to the barn.

The cows stood waiting for us.
The cat meowed and our horse, Brownie, turned his
head when we came in.
The pigs were grunting away in their stall,
and the sheep were bleating in the pen.
Under the roof the hens sat waiting for spring,
when they'd begin to lay eggs again
and be able to go out and scratch in the yard.

We looked Daisy over carefully,
but she didn't seem in the mood to give birth.

I helped with the milking
while John and Allen cleaned up
and took hay down from the hayloft for the cows.
Then we went into the big house
where Mother served the morning meal.
Jesse was up and he told us all once again
about his horrible experience the night before.

Later, when I was on my way to school,
I looked around a few times.
But I didn't see any wolves.
White rabbits ran past, disappearing into the snow.
In the trees finches and sparrows were fluttering
about; there were still
some rowanberries left on the branches.

When I left school in the afternoon,
it probably wasn't colder than twenty degrees.
The sky was cloudy and a wind had started up.
As I came into the forest, I heard the sounds
of an ax.
I followed the tracks of our sled,
and soon I found myself beside Father and Nathan.
They were busy cutting down small birches
that we'd use for firewood next winter.

I went over to pat Brownie,
and just then the first snowflakes began to fall.
In two minutes the air was completely white with
snow.
Everybody, including Brownie, shook with worry.
"That's all for today," said father.
"Nathan, see that you have all the axes,
and, Ollie, you help me load the sled."

It couldn't have taken more than a half hour
for us to get out of the forest and onto the road,
but in that time the wind had grown into a storm.
The snow came swirling over the glades and meadows
and whipped us in the face so hard it stung.
But Nathan and I laughed. We whooped and screamed,
when suddenly a crash was heard.
A big pine tree had fallen down near the road,
taking several other pines down with it.

Brownie became nervous. Just as father was about
to push on, we heard another crack somewhere
nearby. We drew close together, Nathan and I,
while the cracking sounds became more violent.
With a thundering crash,
a big fir tree fell to the ground
just inches in front of Brownie's nose.

When we finally got the fir tree out of the way, with
the help of axes and saws,
Nathan and I didn't think it was fun anymore.
We looked fearfully at the swaying trees that stood at
the edge of the forest.
I thought about the bear that lay asleep in its den.
If it had its home just under a spruce that was falling
down, maybe the roof would cave in,
and then the bear would come lumbering out, sleepy
and irritable.

Suddenly we saw four elks coming
almost straight for us.
They must have been on their
way into the woods to find
protection.
Blinded by the snow and the
wind, they didn't see us until
they were nearly in front of us.
Then they disappeared in between
the trees.

By the time we'd unloaded the birch logs
and gotten the sled into the carriage shed,
we were so tired we could hardly talk.
John and Allen were busy plowing a path to the barn.
Father told them about the elks and the fir tree
while Nathan and I led Brownie off to his stall.

The snowstorm was howling even louder
when we came back into the barnyard.
Not once did I see those small mice that usually peek
out from the sides of the house.

Mother was glad to see me.
She'd been so worried.
Of course, she didn't know that I'd met up with
Father and Nathan in the forest.

When we learned that Jesse had gone on his way,
Nathan and I became worried.
Jesse would never be able to make it through such a
storm.
And so Nathan was allowed to go along with me
to look for Jesse.

We took Brownie from the barn and set out on the
road.

When we had gone quite a distance,
Brownie suddenly shied back and climbed down into a
ditch.

When I looked up, I saw a lynx
curled in an oak tree just thirty feet in front of us.
Both Nathan and I screamed as loud as we could,
and the lynx disappeared into the snow.

Nathan got Brownie up out of the ditch again,
and we pushed on in the snowstorm about an hour
before we met up with poor Jesse.
He was on his way back to our place.
Now he was happy and grateful to ride with me on
Brownie
while Nathan trudged through the snow.

In the evening when it came time to milk the cows,
the drifts reached halfway up the house.
Daisy was obviously going to give birth soon,
so Nathan and I stayed out in the barn.
The storm howled as if it wanted to tear off the roof.
The pigs, sheep, and hens were completely silent.
We waited a few hours. Nathan had fallen asleep
when Daisy finally started to get up.

A quarter of an hour later the calf was born.
Daisy licked it clean and then suckled it.

It was very cold in the barn.
A cloud formed in front of our mouths whenever we breathed.
"The calf will freeze in here tonight," I said.
We found an old blanket,
which we wrapped the calf in,
and then we headed out into the storm.
Finally we made it to the big house with the calf.
Grandma said, "Now that's a real storm calf."
Later, we christened her Stormy.

Two days later the air was still and cold.
It was surely twenty below.
Father and Nathan were busy plowing the road.
I took my skis and went to school;
I was glad to be back among people again.

But Stormy remained in the big house
far into the month of February.